Hamlet's Knot

Collected Poems

By

Lawrence Bullock

Hamlet's Knot copyright 2013
Lawrence Bullock
All Rights Reserved
ISBN 978-1-300-43149-7

First Edition

For Fred and Jack

Contents

The Murder Minutes……6
Stinking Up the Joint……7
Cleaning the Roof……8
Black Cat At Sea……9
I Think I Wrote This……10
God Made Me……11
Maneuvers……12
Sunny Day……13
Oh My Love……14
Belief……15
What I've Killed……16
We Go Back……17
Hamlet's Knot……18
Wish List……19
American Guns……20
For The Record……21
The Kennel……22
A Guide……23
The Path……24
Epater le Bourgeois……25
A Pastoral……26
Race Car Race Car Race Car……27
The Far Away……28
Just Checking……29
Excuses……30
Sun and Moon……31
Moment……32
When I Say……33
The Pilot's Last Thought……34
Oh……35
Song So Long……36
Repeat As Needed……37
The Headless Poem……38
What I'll Miss……39
Sacred……40
Speak Up……41
Wonderful World……42

The Murder Minutes

Maybe there was blood washed down
the drain. Maybe the knife scraped bone.
Maybe the skin was peeled back.
Tossed into a brown paper sack.

Maybe they were pulled from their home.
Maybe children, maybe older, alone.
Maybe the smell of them burning
produced some primal pagan yearning.

Maybe once we looked below the surface.
Maybe we stank of laughter and murder.
Maybe we crossed our fingers, wishing,
tossed our lines, continued fishing.

Stinking Up the Joint

Man, he says, some people are half
dead and some people are half baked.
I can't make heads nor tails of their
minds and I don't think they can either.

I love living, I'll tell you with truth
in my heart, I don't believe you ought
to be sad because you got that first
big chance when you squirted out.

Now maybe you had it tough, huh,
who ain't, it's all tough, coming down
that slick alley was tough, you couldn't
breathe, but you did, headfirst.

Nobody ought to listen to me cause
I'm nobody, but hey, I'm alive, I'm
kicking, I'm hangin' in. I'm on fire
and I ain't stinking up the joint.

Cleaning the Roof

Every year a needled carpet, banked
against the skylights, must be dealt
with. As chores go, it is ultimately ranked
in the body steeply, and is deeply felt.

Race the sun before it beats and butters
you, burns the skin, heats to slick sweat,
outrun it. A stellar jay's feather flutters
off the roof's edge. Remember: there's no net.

Scrape moss down to the gray shingle,
anticipate decay, fling the matted bits
away, Hear that stellar jay. It's wing'll
never miss the feather. There it sits.

It must know I can't fly. Such a long way
down. Twenty five feet will kill you, yes,
it will. But the work fulfills the day.
The roof is clean. The jay is not impressed.

Black Cat At Sea

Softly sadly sincerely, I, Black Cat, say
to the moon: It is a great sorrow for you
to be so lost.

Night air will damage my fur or my
whiskers , meow, let me enter the house,
Let me enter now.

The rat waits and is not afraid . Look at my
teeth. It will not survive. Or at least
I hope so.

If I cross your path, it is unlucky. Puny
human, watch your step. I will take
you down with me.

Meow. Meow. Closer. Closer. Yes,
it is all as planned. I love the fingers
on your hand.

I Think I Wrote This

I think I wrote this poem once before,
because, you know, the stuff is there,
and it's not like I'm some half-wit bore,
but I wrote this poem before. Beware.

There's a room. There's some furniture.
A rug, a skeleton, a bottle of baby tears,
harvested in a nursery. I was drunk, sure,
they say drinking that shit gives you years.

I think I knew what I know now, long
before I really knew it, before I blew it,
I wrote this poem before. Is that wrong?
Don't you love me anymore? Screw it.

God Made Me

Yes, she did, and I was made
of chocolate originally. But I
melted, you see, I melted.
Then another god made me.

I was made from diamonds
then. I was hard and cold.
Stolen to finance a dissolute
lifestyle, lost, lost, at sea.

The third god to make me
made me out of mud. That
was a laugh and a half. I was
blown to pieces in Vietnam.

God is made by me to make
me, god made me to make
god, who made me to make
god. And that is who I am.

Maneuvers

Today in history becomes the mountain top
and I have set my shoulder to the stone.
I like women, I like leather, I like leather women.
I like them when they let me pull their wishbone.
In history we learn that the tide changes daily,
that one must be on one's toes, alert, shifty.
I like women, I like ice cream, I like ice cream women,
I like them when they're lean and mean and thrifty.

History is a plate filled with shrimp, shellfish,
because history eats lower on the food chain.
I like women, I like it when they're selfish,
I like them absolutely impossible to train.
Today in history we learn to maneuver around
the battlefield, to walk in peace among the free.
I love women, I love their smell, their sight, their sound,
I love their wishbones, tides, and ice cream history.

Sunny Day

It's beautiful here. It's very beautiful.
Everyone has a beautiful smile. Everyone.
The sun is out. We are so happy. All.
I ride my dolphin to work in the mine.
It sings to me with a voice so fine.

The day begins with a wonderful song.
We don't know the words but the tune.
We hum the tune, imagine the words.
The sun is out, and the sky is so blue.
The sky isn't sad though, neither are you.

Say the good thing on your mind.
The good word, the good deed, the good.
The good ship is sailing to the good land.
Polish the deck, clear the scuppers.
Say hooray for the mopper-uppers.

It's beautiful. It's terribly beautiful.
So beautiful. It could not be more.
But it will be. It will be more beautiful.
Because I will it. It will be so sunny.
The rain will be afraid. That's so funny.

Oh My Love

The dangerous cloud made its way
to the corner, smiled and crossed
the street. We were in love today.
You wonder, idly, if I have flossed.

Mixed tensions, mixed emotions,
mixed tenses. The world came
from rocks azoic, then explosions
or something. There's no blame

here. Or,rather, don't blame me.
I am a dangerous cloud, making
my way to the corner, the same me
as I always was, so heart breaking.

Belief

I believe in the right moment, done to a turn
in time's hot oven, yearned for, served fresh

to hunger then pulled away. Don't let it burn
you. I don't believe in putting marks in flesh,

let life do that. Scars. I believe in sweat, great
gushers of it during sex, rolling in the wild stink

of it, the scent of the body leaving chance to fate,
the death of everything including the kitchen sink.

Here's to believing or not believing. To care
or not caring. Here's to the universe, all of it.

I believe that you will do what you must do. I dare
you to. I wrote this poem for you. I love it.

I forgive myself for dying. I forgive you, but what
is there to forgive? I believe that we must not believe

too much. Oh, what is believing? What is not?
It's something that you wear upon your sleeve.

What I've Killed

Time, of course. Then there are those small lives
I only think about in passing. I walk through air.
I walk through walls of air. I kill air to thrive,
for me to be, but was it ever really there?

Those small lives. Some I remember so well.
Some I couldn't if you staked me to the fire.
Oh hell, murderer me, I killed you too, do tell.
I kill myself in moments when I should inspire.

Also, millions of mosquitoes, ants, frogs, fish,
spiders, tadpoles, but: not a single dog or cat.
Not me, no budding socio, although I do wish
you'd leash that beast. Yessir. I truly do wish that.

We Go Back

We go back, we go way back, when afternoons
were orange and evenings grey. When 45's spun,
needles dropped, socks hopped. Water balloons
were the weapon of choice. All in good summer fun.

We go back when grief was relief, not entertainment,
solemn ceremonies quiet, subdued, silence healed.
In the heart there was a voice of much revealed intent,
when neighborhoods were such the sword and shield.

We go back, but we can't go back. Ahead, then
with a simple nod to things lost to forward motion.
We go back, there to there, return, begin again.
We stop at time strewn shores. Then cross the ocean.

Hamlet's Knot

I will not ask you, empty head
to help rid me of Hamlet's knot;
he became mad. As Lenau said
one can't ask Death to write the plot.

--Michael Kilby

"*Save me,*" says the body. "*Kill me,*"
says the mind. Sleep, sleep, my
angel, fold your precious wings.

Be of good cheer. Accentuate
the positive. "*Oh dear, what can*
the matter be," the doctor sings.

Let us rest in the cool shadows,
our cocktail casual face caressed
by cruel anguish, fool's gold

teeth smiling, discerning rictus,
beguiling and beguiled. Let us
rest in shadows, cool until cold.

"*The only serious philosophical*
question," says the Stranger,
"*is the end, where, why, how.*"

"*Save me,*" says the body, "*let us*
end in jest." "*Why not,*" (persistent mind)
"*Oh why not, angel, now?*"

Wish List

Once again I witness the descent into fall,
mourn the astilbe gone ragged, thin flower
nestled near toy maples, smell the fine misted
fog become drizzle, sense the death hour.

Become myself as I was when I was
young, beholden to dry and dusty leaves,
sepulchres of whimsy, grand tombs of fun,
what summer gives us and winter receives.

Could I leave this all behind, much less to say
than thought, with a hey nonny, nonny, no.
My wish list: All good things, my bonny, for you,
for yours. As I would always wish it so.

American Guns

American guns don't take no guff.
They're tough. They paint sunsets,
my pets. Look at them smoking,
joking. It's so thought provoking.

I said sunsets. The purple skies,
the sun dies. The moon weeps,
mah peeps. American guns shoot,
reboot. Atten-shun! Now salute.

Arm us with guns, American
ones. Shiny pistols, like Swarovski
crystals. Go ahead, ask the dead.
American guns, in God we dread.

For The Record

In time it stinks that time takes
what time gave, to our delight.
My heart breaks out the champagne,
cries itself to sleep all night.

I wish I had a cigarette, no, no,
I wish I was a cigarette, smoked
by Bob Dylan, in that old movie,
the black and white one, where he joked.

Once that was over, the minutes
you loved me were gone, transferred
those moist moments to a rusty dumpster
behind the Children's Theatre of the Absurd.

I wish a heroin habit had me, no, wait,
I wish I was heroin, a bleeding hero
flying through Keith Richard's veins
although he's clean now, don't you know.

Things leave you: Time, love, muscle,
the light fades, needle hits black vinyl,
snap, crackle, Pops. I love myself, I do,
I do. And you do, too, and that's final.

The Kennel

Standing on the always earth,
to never fear the day away,

watching the flight of bees and birds
who never kneel and never pray,

the sun shines on the rich and poor,
who tolerate each other, yet

each knowing nothing is for sure
short sell the rain to hedge their bets.

Barking behind the kennel gate,
the unloved poor can see the sky.

They beg for scraps, roll over, wait
for love. For love. Until they die.

The always earth, it gives, it takes.
Oh lord, the promises it makes.

A Guide

Here's how to read me: Step one. Breathe.
Take a deep breath. Again. Now, read

the line once through. The line, not your intent
which is all you. That is not what I meant.

Each line, for the sound, for the gut twist.
Take a deep breath. Now, touch your wrist,

feel the pulse. It may match. If not, look
again, at the words, at the beat. It took

me time to write this. So what. Yet
we make so much of athletic sweat.

Never mind. To continue. Remember: I
love you, though I have forgotten why.

To wrap up, it rhymes because, because,
this is a business and these things have laws.

The Path

The path is strewn with peafowl feathers, which,
I can't remember why, have always reminded me
of Flannery O'Connor, who raised peacocks,
peahens, who practiced a faith solid and secure,

limited by a knowledge unlimited, who brought
a world to life from her body's landscape. From
what I've read, she was polite, even in anger.
I've admired her forever. As to those peafowl

feathers: They are in my imagination. I want
to see them. Flannery would hate that. She
might chide me and say, *Now, you're making*
that up. And where do you go from there?

She would be right. This poem began with
a lie. It will not end with one, as many journeys
do. Oh soft and gentle lady, I am a fool,
but I am kind, I am feckless, but not cruel,

I am a fool but I have faith in what is true.
The path is strewn with sunrise, kisses,
caresses, dreams, the bliss of knowledge
and the near misses of our useless wrath.

It does not end with this. It does not end.
I will not pretend to know where it does end.
The path is not the path, we are not done.
The path is hard, and harder, once begun.

We create the world each day, as an author
might. Like Flannery O'Connor, whom we read,
think, that's the world I live in, the savored
grace of the imagination. Then turn out the light.

Epater le Bourgeois

Your laziness insults the dreaming creature you are most like
and connects you with a presence that is positively ghost-like
in a way that drops such havoc in drab and dreary lumps
on what are formally or normally considered toxic dumps
that have for some become such tidy homes for tidy folk
who are the forlorn punchlines of a obscure dirty joke.

I stretch out beside the opium pipe of my own good intentions
playing with my Victorian collection of decadent inventions
that I was sure would better worlds I must have then created
only to destroy them on a whim, as I have often stated
when I am asked . Come, come, come, learn from my dark
eyes. Sit down. You must speak forcefully to make a solid mark.

I would like to write a knife into your nested heart
that would remain in place, my dear, for love, for life, for art,
to serenade you sweetly with a dismal fog horn trill,
(I must admit, and then deny, that would give me a thrill).
I know exactly why someone like me was so designed:
To stare, and stare, and stare, and stare, and stare, ‘til I go blind.

A Pastoral

The green field has several cows in it.
I enjoy cows. They don't ask for much.
The sky is blue. That's good, too.
When it's not blue it's usually grey.
See that bird? Do you know what it is?

Me neither. Yes, you're blind. I forgot.
Look out for that hole. I can't carry
you. Here, touch this cow. Yes, it's
a cow. Don't step in that oh shit,
too late. Well, I said I was sorry.

I will not clean your shoe. I will not.
You're not helpless. You've told
me you're not. Look, I don't want
to argue anymore. OK. OK. Then
find your own way home. It's east.

I will. I will have a good time. In fact
I'll probably have a better time
than you. I'm going to hop this fence
now. And it's not a cow it's a
bull. Wish I'd sold tickets to this.

Race Car Race Car Race Car

Who is you and where does I when all
is said and done. Dust or flesh or star
shine with great hope. If you should fall,
may you heal with such rich roadmap scar.

I sleep sound in a bed of rose thorns
scented lightly with faux martyrs' tears,
starter fluid, a sound of angel's horns
stalled on the track, as they strip their gears.

I dream of grease-monkeys, oil apes
of a driven bent, I, instantly awake,
fed almonds by Greek slaves, grapes,
for that hunger which I fast to break.

Who is I and where does you begin?
Who does this read when it sees the soul?
I sure you wish for something always when.
How start again when the engine's cold?

The Far Away

I ride on top of the opalescent breeze
to knit the shadow world together.
There is a smile tree that sheds leaves
in heaps suitable for jumping into.

My hair is golden, my strength is unlimited,
I wish for things, they instantly appear.
I wear spider webs of possibilities and luck
to the great grand ballrooms of opportunity.

Since I became transparent I have made
too many friends. They bring me food.
The rough wind cannot touch me. Love
is my shield, I have no use for a sword.

When I was a child there were no dreams,
now they flower all around. Look, look. See
where we have come from. See where
we are going. I have vanished into a return.

Please come to visit more often, I wish
you were my left arm, I breathe under
water, we float through the sky. Do you
ever wonder what I look like? So do I.

Just Checking

The room, the shirt, the look, the air,
the limitations of the body, where
an arm goes, or a leg, placed there,
a lack of concentration, or of care,

where we begin, or end, or find
the chair as it meets our fat behind,
and, somewhere further north, the mind,
which gets lost sometimes, goes blind,

having caught Head Up Ass disease
spread by many as they try to please
everyone, like me, minor poet, tease,
long winded with this labored wheeze.

Just checking in, just flexing the pen,
just putting my sexy finger in the wind,
to see which way it blows, my friend,
the real, which is pretty much pretend.

Excuses

I was going to. I can’t. Here’s why:
Suffer little children, and then die.

I got the motor, got no wheel.
Well, well, some say nothing’s real.

I’m kind. That’s cool. Seriously.
Everything slides right by me.

Tick tock. That’s time. But then:
Next week. Next year. The end.

Sun and Moon

If you travel to the sun, do so at night, haha.
Otherwise you will burn to a black crisp.
When I was eleven, I think, I heard that joke.
The guy who told it to me had a lisp.

So it came out, *thun*, and kids are cruel.
All differences are alchemized to shame-fuel.
Yes, it was shameful, yes, we weren't bright.
That guy. I sure hope he turned out all right.

I don't know many jokes about the sun.
I don't know that many jokes about the moon.
There may be some. I haven't told one.
Jump right in. Please. Have some green cheese.

Man in the moon says to the Sun, *Yo, dude, yo.*
You're two faced. Me, I stick to one most days.
Sun says, *You're a pale reflection of me, so*
chill, moon. You're just going through a phase.

I beat up that kid who told me the sun story.
That's why he's in this poem. His name? Don't know.
I hope I don't end up in purgatory.
Oh what the hell. It was so long ago.

Moment

The moment before sleep was the rebirth
of Christ, when he questioned his own worth,
ours too, which he assumed, along with sin,
worn to Golgotha, like a second sexy skin,

then was nailed, blah, blah, blah, and so on
and so on (it's wearying how some people go on).
Anyway, that moment before sleep, delicious
as a Georgia peach, and fuzzy too, nutritious.

That blissful moment when the mind lets go
of Christ, of peaches, of everything you know,
a sort of death really, without really dying,
a high wire act that is so death defying.

A moment not to be confused with the moment after,
when there may be screams, or maybe laughter,
inside the dreams, ridiculous or focused,
with Maxfield Parrish clouds, or clouds of locusts.

Ah well, both can be useful. I'll bet Jesus,
when he wasn't getting nailed, blah, blah, to please us,
had that moment, (and later on the doubt one).
Christ. Saviors. How'd we ever live without one?

When I Say

One thing I think of nearly all the time is death.
Doesn't mean I'm morbid or weird.
I wrap myself in the black flag of my death
to come. I'm skeered ma, really skeered.

Another thing I think of is food. Don't eat
as much as I used to. Used to eat, and all
the time. Never got fat. Nope. Never.
Now I do. Good thing I'm reasonably tall.

I used to think about sex more than dying.
It was a large part of my lusty charm.
I used to eat during sex. Yes, I meant that.
I meant eating *that way*. Don't be alarmed.

Oh what's the use. Here's the use. Here's
the goddamned use. Let me softly tell you
what the use is. You need to know so
here is it: Sorry. This poem is done, too.

The Pilot's Last Thought

As I approach the landing site I note that
the loose aggregation of winged birds

is unusually large. They almost seem to
be aiming for me. Of course that's absurd.

That's paranoia. I'm tired. It shows, I think.
The screaming has abated. It's so quiet.

I spread out around the waistline of my
self, content with my less fashionable diet.

My wings are iced, my tea is spiced,
the lights of the city wink like bait

fish in a sunlit ocean wave. Touchdown.
No one around. I am too early, or too late.

My plane becomes a dragon. As I turn,
I face its fiery breath, and start to burn.

Oh

There was a sunset that I put in my pocket
where it burns, it burns. You can't wish
for a miracle unless you are willing to accept
it. Look. Look. Thousands every day.

The one you want is still a million miles
away. That's too bad. It's all right. Please
be aware. There is no such thing as a mistake,
just a truth that drifts outside the lines.

So many things to do and so much time
to do them. Life is not short, it is not long,
it never wanted to thrill you with its brilliance
or shame you for being wrong.

Come on. Let's skate this pond before
it melts, let's swim this lake before it dries,
let the mountain come to you, let
the ocean break inside. Oh. Find your eyes.

Song So Long

Where are your shoes? On your feet.
Where is your mind? Laughter, laughter.
I got the blues today. That's neat.
I hope I don't forever after.
I hope I sing a song that's true
I hope I can come back to you
I hope I hope and then I hope
What will I have for dinner?

Who cleans the house? Is it you?
Why take pains when you take care.
What's it mean to be past due
When the present doesn't share
I hope I make a sound that's clean
I hope I'm nice and never mean
I hope I hope and then I hope
Where is my lonely lover?

Who'll place me in the final hole?
Who'll cry and dance and then forget.
Who'll swear I had a loving soul,
my portrait paint in silhouette.
I hope I travel far to find
I hope I see you when it's time
I hope I hope and then I hope
I'm being born tomorrow.

Repeat As Needed

Bang. You're dead. How did it feel?
Where did you grow up? Were your
parents alcoholics? Do you favor
that new pop star? Wow. Just. Wow.

We make things so gosh-darned real
it seems we need more and more
like the bubblegum that loses flavor
on the bedpost overnight. How

does America feel now that death
comes like a drunken milkman
with a quart of tragedy every other
month or so? America, please speak

into the microphone, your breath
makes me cringe, but I'm a real fan.
If you were here I'd be your lover,
at least until sometime next week.

The Headless Poem

It was a dark and stormy night. Ha ha.
I'm not going there. It is dark, though.

But that's always the case. Tra la.
Without my head I walk, but I walk slow.

I want to hold your hand. There. It's
out where we can see it. Rather, feel.

But I have no head, ergo, no wits.
My dark and stormy night. So real.

What I'll Miss

I think about dying and wonder how *you* will
and I'm terrified or under the impressions
become flesh, which can be seen in life's land fill
where the beastly priest takes trash confessions.

What I will miss is this, as Williams said, words,
as if all worlds were there, said Creeley, grand
one-eyed raconteur among the lesser turds,
who pulled the air apart, you understand.

Words, words, words. You know. The sad Dane
said it three times, that's the rule for plot.
I'd like to spend a day in Shakespeare's brain.
That's all for me. So, what the hell you got?

Sacred

We don't know who we are, beg
for instruction, please make us
whole from pieces, to powder-keg
blows: some explosions break us.

Howl down the wall of being,
see the empty room where that
debatable all purpose all seeing
creature waits like a shit house rat.

Oh my where we were to go
for many moons a solo crow flies,
to better ways they say, this was so
in olden days, no, no, that was lies.

I lose, I sink down where I am but hark
back hill to hill as sunset burns
away the day. Life is always stark.
The sacred sunrise soul of me returns.

Speak Up

A breeze may sit in a chair properly or not
to shoot itself. What did I say to you. What.

Sit down. You may speak that way to God
but in my house you must not. You're so odd.

Another wrinkle mapped me, I tapped
myself on the shoulder, said Boo! Snapped.

The amazing thing about life is: Damn.
I forgot. Don't point. Who's next? I am.

Wonderful World

It’s been good to us, this wonderful world
with water to drink, plants and animals
to eat, things underneath that shine, that
we kill each other for, and, oh, television!

It’s been floating in its own juices
for some time now. It will go on and on.
There may be more like it somewhere.
That’s a fun thought. More wonderful worlds.

Truthfully, it is a wonderful world.
It’s never lied to us. It doesn’t cheat
at cards, steal, bully, gossip, rape anyone.
It will hold us like needy babies until we die.

I imagine it thinking, *Who are these
creatures? Did I make these? I suppose
I did.* Then I imagine the wonderful world
sighing, singing itself softly to sleep.

www.ingramcontent.com/pod-product-compliance
Ingram Content Group UK Ltd.
Pitfield, Milton Keynes, MK11 3LW, UK
UKHW041904190726
13854UKWH00003B/1083